A COLORFUL CASE OF STOLEN ART AT THE GALLERY

AN EMILY CHERRY COZY MYSTERY

BOOK SIX

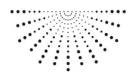

DONNA DOYLE

PUREREAD.COM

CONTENTS

CHAPTER ONE

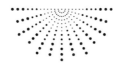

"Oh, good! You're here!" Lily Austin jumped up from behind the front desk of Best Friends Furever and took Emily by the elbow as she brought her back into the office. "I couldn't wait for you to get here this morning!"

Emily Cherry felt her cheeks color with the flattery. "I like to think my little blog posts about the animals you have up for adoption do work fairly well, but I don't think I'm that much of a celebrity." Her blog had been her main hobby in recent months ever since she'd retired from Phoenix Insurance and realized she needed something else to occupy her time. Emily had been experimenting with different topics for her blog, but the one thing that remained constant was her love of animals. She'd made an effort to feature adoptable animals regularly in the hopes that they might have a better chance of finding a home.

Lily laughed. "You do much better than you think! I've got someone who's very eager for his photo shoot today." She led the way into the dog kennel and stopped in front of a cage holding a beagle with big, friendly eyes.

"Oh, hello." Emily knelt down in front of the chain link and held out her hand, wanting to give the dog a chance to get to know her before she spent some time with him. She liked to put in some real volunteer hours here at Best Friends Furever when she had the chance, and she knew how shy dogs and cats could be after spending time out on the streets and then coming to live in a strange place with so many other animals. The beagle slowly moved up to sniff her hand through the wire. "What's your name, little guy?"

"This is Finnegan." Lily unlatched the door after she'd given them a minute. "He's very well behaved, so much so that I'm really not sure why he's here at all. I can't imagine that anyone wouldn't want him."

As though to prove her point, Finnegan patiently waited inside his kennel even though the door was open. His big eyes stared up at Lily, waiting for permission or perhaps a command. When Lily pointed at her own feet and told him to come, he immediately trotted forward and sat down at her feet.

"Will you look at that!" Emily shook her head. "Poor little thing. I have to wonder what might've happened that someone would turn a sweet little guy like this out on the street."

Lily grabbed a leash from a rack on the wall and opened a side door that led into a dog run.

It was normally a green space full of grass that made a very nice backdrop for photos, but the chilly winter temperatures had things a bit brown and muddy. It would have to do. "I agree. The thing is, there are probably any number of wonderful animals out there who are equally deserving of a good home, but we simply don't have the space. We're a very small shelter, and I'm starting to have to turn animals away."

Emily's heart ached as she snapped photos of Finnegan, sitting, shaking Lily's hand, and spinning in a circle. "I suppose you don't really have the space here to put in more cages."

"No, but a friend of mine is in construction, and he could build an addition at cost. That cost is still rather prohibitive, considering we're operating paw to mouth around here. That's actually why I'm so happy to see you today. The Stevens Fine Art Gallery has agreed to work with us on a fundraiser, and I was wondering if you could help me with some of the arrangements."

"Oh, the place right across from Daydream Café? I've seen it, but I haven't been in there." Emily bent to the side to get a better picture of Finnegan's cute little face, and she immediately regretted it when her back twinged. She could easily get caught up in the moment, but she wasn't as young as she used to be! "I'll do whatever I can."

"They're holding an art raffle," Lily explained as she took a rubber bone out of her pocket and chucked it across the yard. Finnegan took off after it, his ears flapping. "Local artists have agreed to put their pieces on display, and the gallery will hold a big event where the public can come in to buy tickets. All the proceeds come to the shelter, which is very generous of Mr. Stevens. There won't even be all that much work for us to do, but I'd love some help with finger foods and table decorations."

Emily tipped her head as she thought about this. She'd never had an experience quite like this before, where someone had put her in charge of part of a charity event. It was certainly a cause that she wanted to support though, and even if Lily had asked her to paint a masterpiece, she was sure she would've found a way to do it. "I'd be happy to."

"You're wonderful, Emily," Lily enthused as she patted her thighs and encouraged Finnegan to cone running back to her. "I'll be spending my time ordering the raffle tickets and trying to get the word out for the event, and I wasn't sure how I was going to squeeze it all in. The show and the start of the raffle is Friday, so there's not much time."

"No, there really isn't," Emily agreed. It wouldn't be much time at all, especially since she had no idea what she was doing, but she knew she'd get it figured out. "I'll get started as soon as I get home."

That was mostly true, as the first thing Emily did when she got home was actually to put the photos of Finnegan and a little bit of information about him on her blog. "There we are," she said to Rosemary, who sat in the dining chair next to her. "Hopefully, someone will see how wonderful dear little Finnegan is and give him a home right away. I think he'd make someone very happy."

Rosemary licked her paw and ran it over her whiskers, smoothing them into place. They bounced back out as soon as she let go of them, twisting every which way and giving her a rather disheveled appearance, despite the fact that she was constantly cleaning herself.

"You know, I think if I were to have a dog, I'd want it to be one like Finnegan."

Rosemary paused in her ablutions, fixing her big gold eyes steadily on her owner. Her whiskers twitched.

Emily had to laugh. "Don't look so worried, my dear! I know I don't have the space in my life right now for a dog. I'd be hard pressed to find one better than Finnegan, though. Now, let's see if we can't find some great ideas for the art gala. I know Lily didn't exactly call it a gala, and it might not be as fancy as all that, but I like the idea."

She spent some time looking up various recipes for finger foods and fancy hors d'oeuvres, bookmarking them so she could go back and find them later. There were far more ideas available online than she'd imagined, and she started to wonder why Lily had trusted her with such a thing. "I wonder what people do when someone is allergic to an ingredient," she mused. "And I don't want anything that has to be put in an oven or warmed up, because that would complicate things."

The notepad next to her on the table was quickly growing with ideas, including what was becoming a list of do's and don'ts for this little party. She had concerns about ingredients, messiness, and how inexpensive the foods would be so that they wouldn't detract too much from the proceeds.

"You know, I think this could make a very interesting blog post." Abandoning her search for the moment, Emily tore off a new sheet and began organizing her thoughts in a way that would help her draft a nice little article. It would give the shelter that much more publicity if she wrote about the raffle, after all. The information was quickly outgrowing just one post.

"Oh, Rosemary!" Emily clapped her hands, startling the cat for a moment. "What if I started writing about party planning?"

The cat gave her a similar look to the one she'd had on her face when Emily had mentioned getting a dog.

"Well, I know I have a lot to learn, but I can do that as I go along, as I do with a lot of other things. I mean, I didn't even know how to have a blog when I first started this adventure, so what's a little bit more research?" Her pen was flying over the paper now as she began generating ideas for future posts. "It seems to me that there's an awful lot that can go into this. General party planning, how to use them for fundraisers, ideas for snacks and décor.

Why, I could even find other recipes or décor ideas online and try them out to let my readers know how well they went. This could give me enough posts for months!"

No longer interested in party planning, Rosemary curled into a tight ball and tucked her nose behind the fluff of her tail.

"Don't worry. I don't plan to start having parties here at the house on a regular basis. It could be kind of nice, though. You know, the kids and their families, or maybe some friends. You don't know this, but Sebastian and I used to invite other couples over for dinner about once a month or so." She smiled as she reminisced about her late husband and the way he'd always been a little bit nervous right before their guests would arrive. "I think he'd be quite happy to try out these little canapes and petit fours."

The cat blinked her golden eyes and then closed them the rest of the way.

"Fine. You go right ahead and pretend to be asleep. I don't think I'll sleep a wink tonight, not if I've got a party to plan and a website to work on!" Emily fixed herself a cup of tea and continued her research.

CHAPTER TWO

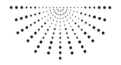

T he rest of the week slipped by far too quickly as Emily bought and tested several different finger foods and fussed over what color of tablecloths to use. She had her little car packed to the gills when she walked into the front door of the Stevens Fine Art Gallery on Friday night.

It wasn't anything like the bigger museums and galleries that Emily had been to in larger cities, but it carried the same quiet air of dignified art, as well as the smell of paint. The walls were tall in the old downtown building, reaching up toward the stamped tin ceiling.

They'd been painted in subtle colors, with a dusty blue here or a deep tan there that accentuated the paintings hung on them. One rather large painting was displayed in the very center of the main room, encased in a gold frame, and displayed on a sturdy easel.

Emily needed to get the food set up, but she paused to study the canvas. It depicted a woman with her back to the viewer. Her head was turned enough to the side that the profile of her face could be seen. Her hair flowed down her back, each one painted individually with what must have been the tiniest paintbrush. These were created in various towns of brown, sienna, caramel, and chestnut, but also what looked like pure gold. The metallic paint had been used to highlight her dress and the windowsill she leaned against. The ethereal look of the painting was something Emily could easily see herself getting lost in.

"I see you've found the star of our show this evening," a deep voice said over her shoulder.

Startled, Emily turned to find herself looking into a pair of friendly dark eyes. His deep olive skin was a contrast to the white hair receding from his forehead. He extended a hand. "I'm Alfred Stevens, the owner of this establishment."

"It's very nice to meet you." Emily juggled the boxes and bags she'd brought from the car in order to shake his hand, and she suddenly felt very aware of her bright red hair. She wondered if perhaps the blue dress she'd put on for the evening's event was too much, considering the subtlety of Alfred's dark suit. "It's so generous of you to put on this event for Best Friends Furever. I know it means a lot to Lily."

Alfred smiled pleasantly. "Ms. Austin is trying to accomplish a lot for the animals in this town, and I can't imagine anyone can do it alone. I can't take all the credit, though. Our lovely artists are the ones who've agreed to let their pieces be raffled off in order to benefit the shelter. The only thing they'll truly get in return is a little bit of recognition that might help boost their renown. That's hard enough in the art world."

Emily gestured at her packages. "I'm here to set up the food. Could you tell me where I should be?"

"Right over here." He led her to a room off to the side. It was as elegant as the main part of the gallery, with smaller paintings displayed all along the wall, and tiny price tags affixed to the frames. "Many of the artists featured in the raffle also have paintings in here for sale, so I'd like to encourage the guests to see everything we have to offer. I should go check on a few other things before the event officially gets started, so please excuse me. Do let me know if there's anything you need."

"Thank you very much." Emily couldn't help but be impressed. She had to force herself to remember that she was in a small gallery in Little Oakley, because it was all so very regal. She busied herself with preparing the refreshment table, but she also found herself constantly looking up at the beautiful art on the wall.

She was still fussing with the canapes and making sure they were all evenly spaced on the table when Lily walked in with Finnegan on a leash. "Oh, it looks wonderful! I can't believe what a nice job you did."

"Do you really think so?" Emily tugged at a corner of the tablecloth to straighten it, and then she fiddled with the stack of napkins. As much as she'd tried, nothing had come out looking quite as refined as the photos she'd seen online in other blog posts and articles. This was purely volunteer work, and the general look would be destroyed the moment someone took the first hors d'oeuvre from a tray, but she wanted it to be as impressive as possible. "I think there are some things I'd change if I had the time."

"No," Lily insisted. "It's perfect. What do you think, Finnegan?"

The dog sat obediently at her feet and thumped his tail against the floor.

"Maybe he's appreciating the wonderful art," Emily joked. "He must have good taste if he's allowed in an art gallery, after all."

"I brought him in to meet Mr. Stevens, and he agreed that he would be the perfect ambassador during the event. Mr. Stevens said he wouldn't normally let animals come into a place like this, but that Finnegan was too polite to say no to."

"I can't say that I disagree." Emily reached down to pat Finnegan's head. "You might find yourself being adopted after everyone gets a good look at you."

Lily checked her watch. "Speaking of which, the doors will be opening soon. Let's head out and see how things go."

Emily followed her back into the main gallery. A table had been set up near the door, where raffle tickets could be purchased. Small stands with big glass bowls had been arranged near each of the art pieces that were available for the raffle. The gallery was as quiet as a churchyard, and Emily felt a knot in her stomach as she worried about whether or not this event would actually bring any funding in for the shelter.

It turned out that she had no need to worry. When Alfred officially opened the doors to the gallery, artists and admirers alike came pouring in. It seemed quite a few people were interested in possibly winning a wonderful piece of art for the mere cost of a raffle ticket, and Emily heard their enthusiasm as she helped Lily sell the tickets.

"It looks like *Moonlight in her Hair* is one of the most popular items of the night," Lily said as she tore off several tickets and handed them to the next customer. "Look at how full the bowl is already!"

Emily looked where she pointed, seeing that the bowl next to the brilliant portrait she'd been admiring earlier was already halfway full. "I can't say that I blame them. It's absolutely gorgeous. I'd consider putting a ticket in for it myself if I thought I had a place to put it. I'm afraid it's a little big for me to put over the mantel."

Lily nodded in agreement. "I know, but the beauty of the painting is probably keeping people from worrying too much about the size of it. I think the money we'll get from that piece alone is going to go a long way toward building that addition."

Emily sighed pleasantly as she watched the local folks mill through the gallery, studying each canvas and sculpture carefully before dropping their tickets into bowls. She'd been worried, but the sheer amount of people here was already proving that it was a success. "I think I'll slip off and grab a few photos, if you don't mind."

"Not at all. I've got Finnegan to keep me company. He's already had five adoption applications today." Lily gently patted the sweet dog's head.

Emily moved through the crowd, taking snapshots here and there. This little event alone was going to be a fantastic post for her blog! She could write about how Mr. Stevens had been generous enough to let them use his space, and how the artists had kindly donated their works. Yes, there was a little bit of a kickback for each of them, in that the people who'd come here tonight for the raffle would know more about the place and might buy one of the other pieces for sale, but it still worked out to a great benefit for the shelter. Having the party in a gallery meant there wasn't much to do for decoration, since the place was already beautiful. There were so many wonderful aspects of this event that she hoped she'd remember them all by the time she sat down at her computer later.

"Oh, excuse me," she said as she bumped into someone while she turned her head to admire a still life. She heard something fall to the floor, and she immediately bent to retrieve the small notebook she'd jarred out of the guest's hands.

"That's all right. I've got it," he said impatiently as he swooped down to grab the notebook. He tugged his driving cap further down on his head and then hurried on to the next painting, one that showed a pastoral scene.

Emily frowned at his back. She hadn't meant to run into him, but he'd certainly seemed offended by the fact that she had. He was jotting something in that little notebook, glancing around the room, and then writing some more. Perhaps he, like her, was trying to remember everything he'd seen tonight so he could write about it later.

The news had apparently gotten word of the raffle, and she spotted several people near the center of the room, holding out their digital recorders as they fired questions at the creator of *Moonlight in her Hair.* "It's Victor Elliott," the man said, straightening his ill-fitting jacket as he spelled out his name for the local paper.

"Mr. Elliott, how do you feel about donating your work to this raffle? It must've taken you quite some time to create this painting."

The artist raised his dark eyebrows at the work in question and nodded. "It did, of course. But you really can't look at it that way when you're creating. It's not like an hourly job, where you simply put in your time and then it's done. Each piece requires its own time. I couldn't even tell you exactly how long this took me, because it was more about capturing the moment."

Emily stood near the edge of the crowd and smiled, seeing how beneficial this entire event had been for the whole community. The artist had an outlet. The newspaper had something to read. Folks would skim the article the next day and wish they'd come. Animals and artwork alike would find new homes. It was simple, but it reached into every part of the community. She loved that.

"You must feel wonderful about the number of tickets that have already been sold for your painting," another reporter commented. "Can you tell us how you feel about that?"

"Fantastic," Victor replied with a grin. "Just wonderful. It's humbling to see how many people are interested in something that I made. There have been times, as I've struggled as an artist, when I began to believe what I'd always been told about art. It was a waste of time. I'd never make any money. There was no point in trying to base my career in paints and brushes. The sheer amount of donations that've been made to the shelter tonight prove otherwise."

"Mr. Elliott, the painting is gorgeous. Is the woman anyone in particular?"

A small smile played over Victor's face. "I'm afraid not. This is something I dreamed up one night, and I simply couldn't forget it until I accurately captured it on a canvas."

Alfred Stevens stepped up next to the artist and put an arm around his shoulders. "I want to remind everyone that the raffle will be open for a full week, so anyone who didn't get a chance to come in tonight can still have the opportunity to own this lovely painting. We're delighted to partner in the name of Best Friends Furever."

Emily's heart warmed as she moved on to peruse the rest of the display. She recognized business owners, friends, and neighbors who'd all shown up. Moving among the crowd, she also noticed the man in the driving cap with the notebook. "Excuse me," he said to a slim young woman who stood proudly next to the embroidered piece that she'd created for the show. "Could you tell me a little bit about this? What do you call this type of work?"

"Oh," she replied, pleasure pinking her cheeks as she glanced at the piece, displayed in its hoop. "It's embroidery on linen."

The man adjusted his glasses and peered closely at the piece. "It's stitches? Did you make all those yourself? Did you do them by hand?"

"All by hand," she replied, dipping her head shyly.

"What a remarkable thing," he muttered, shaking his head. "It almost looks like the little scene is jumping right off the fabric. I've seen plenty of paintings, but I had no idea you could make something so complicated out of a bit of string."

"Actually, it's more than just string," she explained. "Most of the time I use cotton floss, but this one was made with silk. It's more expensive, but it's a true pleasure to work with. It also lays differently on the fabric than cotton."

"Very interesting."

Emily frowned as she walked away. The man had been so rude to her, and yet he was being incredibly polite to the other woman. Perhaps he was much more interested in figuring out which item to use his raffle ticket on than in making friends with strangers he happened to bump into. There was something about him that she didn't quite like, though, and she glanced over her shoulder to get another glimpse of him. He'd stopped talking to the stitcher, but now he seemed to be counting the floor tiles and marking the number in his little book. He was an even stranger character than most of the artists.

Deciding that there were more important things to worry about, Emily returned to the ticket table and helped an interested guest fill out yet another adoption application for Finnegan.

CHAPTER THREE

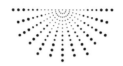

"This is quite the spread," Mavis remarked as she sat down at the dining table two days later.

Emily beamed at her daughter. "Thank you for noticing. I've put quite a bit of work into it. For the blog, of course." The taste of party planning that she'd already gotten simply from helping with the gala had inspired her. Emily had ironed her tablecloth, created a centerpiece, and arranged a vast assortment of finger foods to go with dinner.

"I thought you already tried to blog about food and cooking," Nathan noted as he held out Genevieve's chair for her.

"Yes, but that was completely different. That was all about casseroles and roasts and family meals. Now that I'm focusing on party planning, the food takes on a completely different role. It's important, but it's not the entire focus of things." Emily sat down at the head of the table, feeling quite pleased with what she'd put together. It was only her children who would see it, but they were some of the most important people in her life, after all.

"I think it looks lovely," Phoebe enthused.

Her daughters sat on either side of her, looking equally enchanted.

"Look how tiny the little sandwiches are!" Lucy beamed. She delicately picked one up as though she thought she might accidentally smash it.

"Did a fairy make them?" Ella asked as one was put on her plate.

"No, silly," her sister replied with a roll of her eyes. "Gran made them, and she's definitely not a fairy."

Ella, not wanting to be made fun of by her sister, no matter how reasonable it was, fisted her hands on her hips and stuck out her chin. "How do you know?"

"Girls, that's enough," their father chided softly. "Gran put a lot of work into all this, so eat up!"

Emily chuckled. "It was a lot of work, but it was also quite fun. It's given me many things to write about that I don't think I'll ever get caught up, which is exactly how it want it to be. The raffle has already brought in so much money that I don't think Lily will have a single thing to worry about when it comes to getting the addition built." She felt a warm happiness all over again at the thought.

"It's too bad that beautiful painting was stolen," Mavis commented. "I'm sure that doesn't help things at all."

"What?" Emily's fork clattered to her plate, and everyone turned to look at her. Her eyes, however, were glued on her youngest daughter. "What are you talking about?"

Mavis's lips tightened a little as she realized the mistake she'd made. "You hadn't heard? It was all over the news this morning that one of the best paintings was stolen out of the Stevens Fine Art Gallery."

"Which one?" Emily demanded, even though she already knew.

"I don't remember exactly what it was called. Something about the moon. They had a photo of it on the news, though, and it was absolutely gorgeous."

"*Moonlight in her Hair,*" Emily said with a resigned sigh. She should've known that things couldn't really go that smoothly with a fundraiser. "Oh, this is terrible! That painting was going to bring in a log of money! Lily was counting on it, not to mention all the cats and dogs."

Rosemary, as if sensing how distressed her owner was, twirled around Emily's ankles. She purred softly as she rubbed her whiskers against Emily's leg.

"What's so special about it?" Matthew passed the relish tray, artfully stacked with tiny pickles and olives. "Couldn't the artist just make another one?"

Nathan emphatically shook his head. "Would you ask da Vinci to paint another *Mona Lisa?* I may not know a lot about art, but from a marketing perspective, simply making another one completely diminishes the value of the first one."

"It's not as though he's some famous painter," Mavis pointed out to her brother. "You're not wrong, but we aren't talking about da Vinci or van Gogh. This is a local artist, which honestly makes me wonder why anyone would bother stealing it in the first place."

Emily drummed her fingers on the table, no longer interested in seeing the wonderful arrangements she'd put together and blogging about them. The only thing she could think of was the shelter and how much this would affect them. "Mavis, you said you heard about this on the news?"

Her daughter nodded as she wiped her fingers on a napkin. "It was the biggest story of the morning."

"And did they say anything about who did it or what happened? Did someone break a window or bust through the lock on the door?"

Mavis shrugged. "They didn't give a lot of details. They said the police were investigating. They'd taken some footage of the front of the building, and there definitely wasn't any smashed glass. There was an older gentleman they interviewed, maybe the owner of the place, who said this was done by someone who knew what they were doing. They'll probably re-air the story this evening."

Emily knew that she was right, but she didn't really want to wait around to see what the news had to say. She thumped the side of her fist against the table. "I think I know who did it."

"You do?" Nathan asked cautiously.

"I do," she confirmed. In fact, the more she thought about it, the more solid the idea was becoming in her mind. "You see, I was at that gallery all evening for the party. There were quite a few people there, but it's a small space, and I probably saw every single one of them. I'd say most of them were perfectly innocent, but there was one man who was acting rather strangely."

"What was he doing?" Phoebe asked, her attention fixed on her mother.

Nathan made a derisive noise. "Probably nothing that would actually prove him to be an art thief."

"Except for noting the placement of all the security cameras," Emily replied.

That made her son's mouth fall open, but he snapped it shut again. "You must've been mistaken. Nobody would openly do that."

She shrugged. "I wouldn't have thought so, either, if someone had asked me. But he was acting very strangely. He kept looking around and jotting things down in his little notebook. I thought it was odd, but I assumed he was taking notes on the artwork or perhaps on the event itself. But the more I think about it, the more convinced I am that he was looking at the security cameras and measuring the distance from one piece to another."

Matthew took a drink and set down his glass. "Do you know who he was so you can tell the police?"

Emily's shoulders sagged. "I bumped into him at one point, but I didn't speak to him past apologizing. I don't believe I'd ever seen him before. I might be able to ask Mr. Stevens or Lily if they knew who he was, perhaps by his description, but...wait!" She shot up from the table, nearly sending her chair toppling over backwards as she darted into the next room for her cell phone.

Her family was waiting with wide eyes when she returned, and nobody was eating a thing, not even Lucy and Ella. Emily straightened her blouse, feeling a little odd at making such a scene, and she took her place at the table calmly. "I took a lot of photos while I was there. I'd be willing to bet he's in one of them." She scanned through the pictures, hoping she had more than the back of his head or his elbow in the corner. Finally, she found the perfect shot and held the phone out.

Nathan and Genevieve were the first to see it. Genevieve's blonde brows scrunched together. "That's definitely not an art thief."

"And why not?" Emily asked. She passed the phone off to her left so that Phoebe and Matthew could see the photo, with the girls peering over their elbows.

"Because I know him. That's Bert Lowe. He's a renowned art broker and critic," Genevieve explained. "He buys pieces all the time, curating the best collection, and he lets only the most sophisticated buyers purchase them. He wouldn't bother stealing anything, because he has more than enough money to buy whatever he wants from a small place like that."

The phone had made its way around the table, and Emily looked at him once more. In his bland suit and driver's cap, he didn't look like any sort of art broker to her. Not that she knew exactly what an art broker should look like, of course. Most of what was on her walls had either been purchased at a department store or created by her granddaughters. "Perhaps this man just looks like your Mr. Lowe."

Genevieve shook her head and gave Emily a patronizing smile. "I've been to Bert's studio several times with friends. He's got a fantastic, upscale place on the edge of town. I'm a little surprised to see him at such a small gallery, but he's probably looking for interesting finds by new artists."

Emily still wasn't convinced. This man, Bert Lowe or not, had given her a very suspicious feeling from the moment she'd met him. "If this actually is your art critic, then why was he asking such silly questions? He wanted to know all about embroidery from one young woman. On that, I can understand a little bit. He may not have been familiar with her type of work, even as fantastic as it was. But I also heard him ask if a painting was oil or acrylic. Wouldn't he know that if he's the sort of person you say he is?"

Her daughter-in-law flipped her hand dismissively. "It was probably a way for him to strike up a conversation about a piece and find out more about it without letting anyone know who he was. If they did, they'd want to make their painting sound more special and expensive than it actually is."

Emily wasn't convinced. She was no detective, and she fully understood that the work carried out by Chief Inspector Jack Woods and DC Alyssa Bradley was far more detailed and professional than anything she'd ever done. Still, she'd ended up assisting in a few of the department's cases over the past couple of years, and she was starting to think she had a nose for leads. "Where did you say his studio is at?"

"Oh, out on the edge of town, in that new building that went up last year. It's a very modern place, clean and minimalistic. He's up on the second level, which I'm sure he did so that people wouldn't happen to accidentally wander in while they're looking for other offices in the complex." Genevieve studied her bright red nails and then snapped her eyes back up. "You aren't going to go there, are you?"

Emily put her chin in the air. "I might. I could be interested in some high-end art, after all."

Nathan was looking very uncomfortable, caught between his mother and his wife. He cleared his throat and ran a hand through his sandy hair. "Mother, that really might not be a good idea. You don't want to go accusing some prominent member of the community of stealing a painting. It could make you look very bad, and you really ought to leave this sort of thing for the police."

Pursing her lips, Emily thought about DC Bradley. She and Alyssa had formed a nice friendship, and it all started because the young detective had treated her like a real person when she'd stumbled across a dead body in an alley. Everyone else had acted as though she was old and dotty, a silly elderly woman who didn't have any brains left, but Alyssa had been different. She could certainly call her and tell her of her suspicions, but she didn't want to waste her time if she was wrong. "We'll see."

Nathan cleared his throat and grumbled some more.

"Oh, stop," Mavis chided her older brother. "What do you think she's going to do, tie him to a chair and shine a light in his face until he confesses?"

Now Nathan could direct his ire at Mavis instead of his mother. "Unlike some of us, I'm trying to make sure I look out for our mother. There's no reason for her to go tracking down an art thief, especially when her prime suspect is someone who's so well known in the art community. She'll get laughed right out of his office."

Mavis lifted a stern brow. She was the youngest of the three, but she was never one to back down. "She's much stronger than you think. I know you imagine you're being protective, but there's a fine line between that and suffocating."

"All right, children," Emily admonished. "I'd love to have you fighting over me, but not this way. Let's leave it alone for now. I can call Alyssa and let her know what I think, okay?"

Everyone nodded their heads, still looking a little tense. Well, that was all right. They were looking out for her in their own way, and she knew they probably hadn't always appreciated the decisions she'd made and the lectures she'd given when they were children. The difference was, she was an adult, and she could do whatever she wanted, even if that included tracking down an art thief.

CHAPTER FOUR

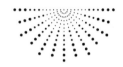

"**A**ll right, explain this to me one more time."

"It's really very simple."

"Yes," Anita agreed. "I suppose it is, except that I thought you were inviting me over here because you wanted my feedback on your next blog post."

Emily smiled in the mirror at her best friend as she touched up her makeup. It didn't sit as nicely on her skin these days as it did when she was younger, and there were times when she chose to go without it entirely, but she felt it was an important part of the effect she was going for. "I do want your honest feedback on that. I know you go to a lot more parties than I do."

Anita patted her smooth gray hair, cut just below chin length and arranged in a sleek bob that made her look younger than she really was. "I suppose that's true, although going to a few more of them might be very good for you."

"So that I can take notes for my blog, or because you don't think I get out enough?" Emily challenged as she picked up a brush and made an attempt at taming her wild red curls. They were shot through with gray these days, but she had a feeling their vivid color would never go away entirely.

"Well, both," Anita admitted. "You're doing much better than you used to, now that you're volunteering at the shelter, so at least I know you're not sitting here in your house all day. A party or two would be nice for you."

"I already went to a party this week, and that's exactly why you and I are going to see this art dealer." Emily slicked on some lipstick, blinked at seeing how bright it was, and dabbed most of it back off.

"Right, that's the part you need to explain again."

Emily laughed a little as she reached into her jewelry box for her nicest pair of earrings. "The painting that was bringing in the most money for the raffle has been stolen, and I'm quite convinced that this art dealer named Bert Lowe was the one who did it."

"Bert Lowe?" Anita had been plucking at her necklace, but she paused as her surprise showed in the mirror. "I've heard of him. He's supposed to be quite the big shot."

"Which is exactly why Nathan and Genevieve don't think he could have anything to do with this, since he could probably afford to buy every piece of art at the Stevens Gallery. I know what I saw, though, and I don't believe he's innocent at all. I don't see anything wrong with making a little trip down to his studio to check him out in a little more detail." Closing her jewelry box, Emily left the bedroom and paused only long enough to pet Rosemary goodbye before she went out the door.

"Won't that be a little suspicious? You can't just walk in and ask him if he did it, and I highly doubt he would have something on display that he'd stolen," Anita pointed out as she buckled her seatbelt.

Emily smiled at she backed out of the driveway. Anita might not understand exactly what they were doing, but she was along for the ride anyway. That was the sort of true friendship that'd carried them through many years. "I won't do anything like that. I'll pretend to be a wealthy widow, interested in some artwork to help me decorate my home."

"At least part of that is true," Anita acknowledged. "I feel as though I need some big sunglasses and a silk scarf to really pull off the part. Or maybe some oversized necklace that no normal person would wear in the middle of the day."

Emily headed across town, feeling a little nervous. "I thought the same thing, and maybe I should've hidden my hair. I'm easier to spot than a lighthouse."

"You look lovely," Anita confirmed as she gripped her friend's hand. "Bert Lowe will take one look at you and decide you're the wealthy, eccentric type who drinks wine out of diamond-encrusted glasses simply because she can."

"You're too kind. Besides, if I had that much money, I'd put the diamonds on Rosemary's collar instead of a wine glass." They had a good laugh over that one, but Emily found that she was only getting more nervous the closer they got. What if Nathan and Genevieve had been right? What if this man was perfectly innocent, and she was making a complete fool of herself? It wasn't as though she planned to actually accuse him of anything. She wanted to see what sort of place he had on the hopes that she might find some sort of clue. Was that really all that crazy?"

"Here we are." Anita glanced in the mirror before turning to Emily. "Are you ready to be one of the wealthiest women in Little Oakley?"

Emily put her nose in the air and looked down it at Anita. "Why hasn't my gold-plated swimming pool been installed yet?"

Her amusement faded as they walked into the quiet office complex. As Genevieve had described, it was a very sleek and modern place. The windows in the lobby were long and slim, reaching almost all the way from the floor to the ceiling. The walls had been painted a pale green, and the carpet was so plush that her feet felt as though they were sinking straight into it. A set of stairs reached up toward the second floor, looking like little more than a few rectangles of metal floating in the air with a curving handrail next to them. They decided to take the elevator.

"Are you all right?" Anita asked.

Emily heard her shaking breaths and knew exactly why she asked. "I'm sure I will be. You know, I've never had such a concrete lead this early on in a case. It makes me nervous that I've gotten it wrong."

"You're getting in your own head because your children have expressed some doubts. The best-case scenario is that this guy falls to his knees, confesses everything, and begs your forgiveness."

That had Emily laughing enough to chase a few of her nerves away. "And the worst case?"

"We get stuck buying some hideous piece of abstract art that makes zero sense." The elevator doors opened, and Anita looped her arm through Emily's. "Shall we?"

The second floor looked very much like the first. They walked down an expanse of hallway, past office doors with the names of their occupants etched in gold lettering. Attorneys, accountants, graphic design firms. Emily had done a little bit of research on the building, and she knew even the tiniest of office spaces here were incredibly expensive. They wouldn't find any dog groomers or daycares in a building like this.

At the very end of the hall stood a heavy wooden door painted black. *Bert Lowe Studio, open by appointment only.* was etched into a small brass plate at the very center of the door.

"If we hadn't been looking for it, I don't think we'd have found it at all," Anita noted.

"I think that was the point," Emily replied. Her hand hesitated as she reached for the knob. They didn't have an appointment, and she wasn't the sort of person to barge into a place and assume that she would be taken care of. That's exactly what an eccentric, wealthy widow would expect, though, so she pushed her way in.

They found themselves in a wide studio that had to be much bigger and far more expensive than the other places that'd been rented out in this building. The long windows had been carried over here, and in between them hung every kind of painting from modern abstracts to what appeared to be antique oils. The walls were a stark white, but the high ceilings had been painted black. Emily moved slowly through the space, expecting Bert Lowe to emerge from behind a wire sculpture of a tree and ask how he could help them. She was fully prepared with her story, explaining how she was looking for that special thing that would make her house really be the life of the party, but there was no sign of the art critic in sight.

"If these things are as expensive as Genevieve says," Anita muttered as she sneered at a splatter of paint on a piece of wood, "then I'm surprised he leaves anyone alone with it all.

You could pick up what you wanted and walk out, and nobody would be the wiser."

"Sssh," Emily warned. "He might overhear, and then our whole act will be for nothing. I wouldn't be surprised if he was the sort of person who eavesdropped on his clients for a while before he actually came out to sell anything to them. That way, he'd already know what they wanted and how much they were willing to spend."

"Smart move." Anita pointed at a narrow doorway toward the back. "Maybe he's back there."

They passed various sculptures, and even high-end furniture, as they made their way to the back of the studio space. They found a smaller room that was mostly taken up with a table. Powerful lights shone down from overhead, and Emily assumed this was where his affluent clients could inspect the details of whatever piece they were interested in. There was no sign of Bert Lowe, however.

"Hello?" Emily called out when they emerged from the little room. "Is anyone here?"

"So much for subtlety," Anita murmured with a smile.

Emily shrugged. "He should've put in a bell or something. This is a terrible way to do business, no matter how wealthy I am."

"Or aren't," Anita reminded her. She poked her head into another small room near the one with the large table. "Um, I don't think Mr. Lowe is very worried about anyone stealing."

"Why is that? Because most of it is hideous?" Emily's confidence was going up, and her nerves were settling. This man was simply being rude, and it was easier to be upset with him for his poor customer service.

"No, because I think he's dead."

Emily peered over her shoulder into a small room of a similar size to the one with the table. It was much darker, and there was a fancy cappuccino machine in the corner. A couch stretched across the back wall. She guessed that the man who lay on it was Bert Lowe. He had the same wireframe glasses and long face as the man she'd run into back at Stevens. The bland suit had been traded out for a loudly patterned silk shirt and trousers, and he no longer wore the driving cap. "Are you sure?"

Anita grabbed Emily's hand as she tiptoed a few steps into the room and leaned forward to peer at the prone man. "I'm pretty sure. I think he's been stabbed!"

Emily's heart clutched as they stepped back out of the room and dialed the police. She noted that they arrived incredibly fast, and she was still reeling as she and Anita waited for the paramedics to finish what they were doing in the small break room where they'd found Mr. Lowe's body.

"Let's have a seat," Emily said, gesturing to a bright red couch that she couldn't imagine anyone ever buying for their home.

"Are we supposed to sit on it?" Anita questioned as she sat down regardless.

"I guess we'll find out if someone sends us a bill." Emily swept her hand across her forehead. "I had this horrible feeling that I was wrong, and I guess I was."

"Now, now." Anita patted the back of Emily's hand. "Don't be so hard on yourself. It was something you felt you needed to know more about, and who knows what might've happened if we hadn't come, or how long would it have been before someone else found him."

"Yes, but to think I was all ready to point the finger at him as an art thief! I can see now how ridiculous it all sounds. I'd call Nathan and Genevieve and apologize to them right away if I didn't also have to admit in the process that I came down here. I hinted that I would pass the information along to Alyssa instead of trying to take care of it myself." Emily leaned forward and braced her head on her hands.

"Speaking of which, your friend isn't here, is she?"

Emily looked up at all the various uniforms buzzing through the place. "I guess not. She must be off for the day. We'll have to put up with Chief Inspector Woods. That'll be a fun one for you." She rolled her eyes as she remembered how condescending he'd been to her in the past.

One of the officers not occupied with dealing with Mr. Lowe was moving around the room, looking for any signs that someone had broken in. He straightened a small painting hanging on the wall, and then he jumped back as the entire section of the wall moved back on its own volition.

Emily, intrigued enough to have forgotten about the disaster they'd found on the other end of the room, got to her feet to move closer. She saw as the officer moved inside that this hidden room was full of more artwork, pieces that looked much more expensive than those openly displayed in the rest of the studio.

"Chief!" the officer called out. "You've got to come and see this! I think this is the piece that was stolen in London last week!"

CHAPTER FIVE

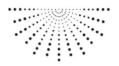

Emily took a deep breath as she got in the car next to Anita a few nights later. "I'm not sure why I agreed to this."

"Because it's good for you, and it might be good for your blog," Anita reminded her as she put the car in drive and sailed off down the street. "This is one of the biggest parties that happens in Little Oakley, and I can't think of any better inspiration for you."

"Maybe, but at the moment it feels like parties, events, galas, or whatever you want to call them, only lead to trouble for me," Emily reminded her, thinking how nice it would be right now to curl up in her pajamas next to Rosemary while they watched some TV together.

Anita snorted. "Well, we might've found a little bit of trouble in trying to track down that missing painting, but think of everything else we found along the way!"

Emily shook her head. "An entire room full of stolen art, items all the way from London, Paris, and New York. It'll take them weeks, or even months, to track it all down and figure out how Mr. Lowe got it, and then they'll be looking for ledgers to see who he sold such things to. A lot of lawyers are about to get their retainers, I'm sure."

"You should be happy," Anita pointed out. "There's a lot of good that came out of your little scheme."

"All that stolen art, and *Moonlight in her Hair* was nowhere to be found," Emily reminded her, still bothered by the fact that, even though she'd been right about Bert Lowe being an art thief, he apparently wasn't the right one. "I suppose you're right, though. I need to let go of it and enjoy this party as much as I can. It's a nice break from how dull and dreary the winter is."

At the country club, Emily found herself completely surrounded by people. This was a much bigger operation than what she'd assisted with at the tiny gallery, and she was impressed by the way the bartenders and waiters were able to keep everyone with a drink in one hand and a snack in another. "I think I'll need to take some notes!"

Anita laughed. "Yes, you should! You won't see it like this any other time of the year, though. This is when they open their doors to pretty much everyone in the hopes of finding new members. They dazzle all their guests with the amazing food, expensive drinks, and excellent service, not to mention the heated pool and the tennis courts. That's not to say it isn't nice to be a member, but it's not quite as fancy as they want to make you think. They just want you to dole out that hefty membership fee."

Emily frowned, but then she quickly turned it into a grin. "That sounds a bit like a fundraiser to me. That makes it even more relevant to my blog!" She jotted some notes down, eager to share this experience with her readers at the earliest opportunity.

Snagging a glass of champagne from a passing waiter, Anita glanced around the room. "At least this silly membership means something. Dan was the one who was always insistent on belonging here, you know. It wasn't really my thing, but he thought it was the only way to truly be considered high class. I pointed out to him that the high fees leave out a lot of wonderful people, but he didn't care. It was the wealthy he was always trying to keep up with, not the kind or the generous. I went ahead and kept the membership after he died, but mostly because the heated pool is so good for these old bones in the winter. You should come with me sometime."

"Maybe." Emily had grabbed a small plate of finger foods and was writing down what was piled on each little cracker and crostini before she tried it. The live music, the crowd, and the mounds of blog ideas around her were quickly making her forget her worries about the missing painting and the funding that was so desperately needed for Best Friends Furever. Suddenly, Emily felt as though she'd finally figured out what she needed to be doing with her life. If she could truly understand how to hold an event like this, one that brought in a big crowd and got people to open up their pocketbooks, then there'd be no end to the amount of money she could raise for the animal shelter or any number of other charities.

She was looking around for more ideas to take note of when she spotted a familiar face. Dressed in a shabby suit, Victor Elliott's face was bright and happy as he chatted with a few other guests. "It was such a disaster. I'm sure I don't even have to tell you," he said as he tented his fingers over his chest. "I'm still completely heartbroken over it, but I suppose I have to accept that this is simply how some things are."

"But didn't you have any insurance on it, if it was worth that much?" one of the ladies in front of his asked.

Emily elbowed Anita in the ribs. "That's the artist who painted *Moonlight in her Hair.*"

Anita assessed the situation. "Those women are on the board. They're very judgmental, and unless they think you'll increase the prestige of the club, you don't have a chance of getting in."

Emily couldn't say exactly what sort of person would increase the prestige of the club. The only thing she really knew about Victor Elliott so far was that he was a painter and that he seemed more than eager to talk to anyone who would listen about his art.

Now, he hesitated a bit as he tried to answer the woman's question. "Well, no. I didn't have it insured. I didn't have any reason to think something would happen to it, you see, and it's about much more than just the monetary value of the painting."

"Yes, I could see that, I suppose," the woman replied doubtfully. "If you'll excuse us, we've got some other people we need to chat with. It was good to meet you, Mr. Ellison."

"It's Elliott," he quickly corrected her. "Victor Elliott."

The women brushed past Emily as they headed to the other side of the room. "Did you see his suit?" one of the commented to the other. "Practically falling apart at the cuffs! He's not going to be able to pay his dues if he can't even get a new suit! Really, Virginia, we've got to start changing how we do these yearly parties!"

Emily glanced over at Victor, who had eagerly engaged someone else in conversation. At least he didn't seem to hear the way they were talking about him, but she couldn't help but feel sorry for him. He was a small-town artist, and he was probably lucky that he had a suit at all, even if it was a shabby one.

She cast her glance to the other side of the room, and her eyes locked on two familiar people. Emily blinked, sure that she was imagining things. Could it really be? It felt so long ago at this point, and maybe she wasn't remembering things correctly, but their faces were etched in her mind from that fateful day. She gripped Anita's arm.

Her old friend instantly knew something was wrong. She broke off the conversation she was having with someone else and turned around. "What is it? What's the matter?"

"You know the day Sebastian died?" Emily whispered. It was a ridiculous question, because of course Anita remembered. "He'd been invited out on the boat with some new friends. He loved boating, and so of course he went."

"Yes." Anita's brow wrinkled in concern as she studied Emily's face. "Right."

"You see those two people over there? Do you know them?"

Anita looked where Emily pointed. "I don't believe so. Like I said, they open this place up to pretty much everyone for these parties."

"They were with him that day." Emily's stomach churned. She missed Sebastian terribly. He loved being out on the water, and he'd been so excited to have a new adventure that day. It had turned into a complete nightmare, and her heart squeezed against her ribs as she stared at the couple. "I remember them very clearly, from when I went down to the shore after the police called."

"We can go if you want to, honey," Anita whispered.

It was tempting, but Emily shook her head. "No, I think I'd like to go and talk to them."

"Are you sure?" Anita's brow wrinkled a little more. "You've been having a nice time, and I don't want you to get stressed out."

"I appreciate that, but I think this is different." Emily couldn't deny that this whole thing with the raffle, the stolen painting, and the dead art thief were indeed stressful, but there were so many things she missed about her husband, and maybe this was a way to have one last connection with them. "I'll be right back."

"I'll come with you." Anita was right at her side as she moved across the room.

The couple had just finished talking to someone else as she approached them. Emily's heart was pounding as she smiled up at them. "Hello. I don't know if you remember me. My name is Emily Cherry, Sebastian's wife."

The man blanched visibly. "Oh. Hello. Yes. I…I suppose I do."

"Forgive me. I don't remember your names," Emily pushed on. She felt ridiculous for being so bold, but it was the truth. Besides, how could anyone expect her to remember the names of some people that she'd only meant once, right after she'd found out her husband had passed away?

"Uh, Dixon," the woman said, extending a hand and pushing her face into a smile. "Annie Dixon, and this is Dillon."

"It's nice to meet you. I mean, I guess to meet you again," Emily replied breathlessly. It was much harder than she'd imagined to come talk to them. There were many days that she could think of Sebastian with nothing but fond memories and warm feelings, but it was different when she was standing here with some of the last people who saw him alive.

"Yes, of course." Dillon dabbed at his forehead, where a bead of perspiration had erupted. "Um, do forgive us, but we've got to get going. We have some other engagements tonight. Shall we?" He held out his elbow.

"Right. Yes. Other engagements. It was nice to see you."

Emily watched them go, and when they'd stepped out through the front door, she realized what a mistake she'd made. "Oh, Anita. I'm so sorry! I didn't even get around to introducing you!"

"Don't you worry about that." Anita dismissed the notion with a wave of her hand. "They obviously weren't interested in talking to us anyway."

"No, they weren't." Emily chewed her lip. She supposed she couldn't have expected them to wrap their arms around her and tell her how nice it was to see her again. They could hardly get out of the country club fast enough, and she'd clearly made them uncomfortable.

Anita put a second glass of champagne in her hand. "Let it go, dear. Let's go have ourselves a good time."

"Yes. Of course. I didn't even make any notes about the decorations yet, and someone really went to a lot of trouble. Oh." She tightened her grip on Anita's arm.

"What is it now?"

"Do you see that woman over there?" Emily had been surprised by the big crowd at the country club, and she hadn't imagined that she would really know anyone here, but she seemed to be seeing familiar faces everywhere. "I think I know her."

"Who is she?"

Emily frowned as she studied the tall woman over near the refreshment table. She had a thin, angular face and big eyes. Her hair was caught up in a knot, with several tresses worked free and curled around her face. "I really don't know, to be honest. I just feel like I know her from somewhere."

Anita took the glass of champagne out of Emily's hands. "I think perhaps you've had enough. Let's get you home and into bed, which is exactly where you wanted to be in the first place."

She'd hardly had any champagne at all, so she knew that wasn't it. She didn't complain as

Anita fetched their coats, though. It'd been a long week, and a good sleep was exactly what she needed. Emily took once last glance over her shoulder, sure that she'd seen that face somewhere before.

CHAPTER SIX

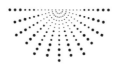

On Friday night, Emily headed back over to the Stevens Fine Art Gallery for the official raffle. She'd worked on her blog quite a bit, and in between she'd managed to get a lot of rest, but she still wasn't feeling completely happy. After all, *Moonlight in her Hair* was still missing.

"Emily!" Lily, with Finnegan on a leash at her side, wrapped her arm around her favorite volunteer. "I'd thought about calling you several times after I'd heard what happened to Mr. Lowe! Someone told me you were the one who found him. Is it true?"

"Well." Emily bobbed her head from side to side, trying to decide how to answer. "I guess I can admit that I had some suspicions about him. I thought I might get a little bit of helpful information if I showed up there, but I'm afraid that doesn't bring back the stolen painting that we've been most concerned for." She looked to the center of the room, where the easel that had once held Mr. Elliott's painting still stood empty. The glass bowl next to the easel was filled to the brim with raffle tickets, not that they did anyone any good at this point.

Lily frowned as she, too, looked at the empty spot. "It's unfortunate, and it means that we can't actually have the drawing for that particular painting. I've spoken with Mr. Stevens, and he's agreed to hold the money in trust for us in case the painting is found. If it isn't, well, then I suppose I'll have to call every person that put in a ticket to see if they want their money back."

"And what about the other pieces?" Emily asked hopefully. "Are the proceeds going to be enough for the addition?"

Pursing her lips, Lily shook her head. "I don't think so. Unfortunately, *Moonlight* was the one thing everyone truly wanted. But we still have a good start, and we can always do another fundraiser of some sort."

"Yes, that's true. I've been trying to learn as much about the process as possible, so it might be something I can help you with." She wondered if Anita would have any good connections at the country club, people with plenty of money to throw around who wanted to make themselves look good. It might be the thing that would help them get past the missing painting, although it wouldn't be a quick solution.

The crowd that'd shown up for the drawing wasn't nearly as big as it'd been on the opening night of the raffle. People milled in front of the paintings, but they no longer looked at them with light and enthusiasm in their eyes. They'd already seen them and paid for their tickets, and even though there were some wonderful pieces here, they weren't as exciting as the brilliant gold tones of Victor Elliott's painting. They had also chosen not to serve any refreshments this time, to save what little bit of money there was coming in.

Even so, the local news outlets had shown up once again as they searched for an update to the stories they'd run earlier in the week. "Mr. Elliott!" one reporter practically shouted. "Do you have a moment to talk?"

Emily was somewhat surprised to see the painter here, since his painting wasn't. He shook his head and waved his hand a little. "I don't really think there's much to say."

"Do you have any idea who might've stolen your painting?" the reporter pushed.

Victor turned as though he was going to walk away, but then he hesitated and turned back. "You know, I really can't say. I only hope they understand how devastating this has been, not only to me but also to the art community as a whole. It makes artists question their passion. As for me, I'm not sure if I'll ever paint again. I'm simply too devastated to think about it right now."

Emily turned her head as she thought she spotted the same familiar woman she'd seen at the country club party, but then Alfred Stevens gently wrapped his hand around her elbow. "Ms. Cherry, I wonder if I could engage your assistance. I think it would be a good idea to have several different people do the drawings, so that it will all be fair. We're going to start in a few minutes. Perhaps you can help me with this first one?" He gestured toward a still life of apples.

Only a small pile of tickets sat in the bottom of the bowl, and it made Emily's heart plummet. Still, she forced a smile. "Of course. I'd be delighted."

The drawing went off without a hitch, or at least no more of a hitch than the initial theft had already caused. Emily, Lily, and several other volunteers from the audience helped draw all the winning tickets, and the main gallery was emptied out by the end of the night.

"It looks strange in here now," Lily commented, frowning again as she glanced toward the vacant easel in the middle of the room.

Mr. Stevens, however, saw it all in a much more positive light. "A freshly bare wall is exactly what you want in a gallery, though! It means I have the chance to put something else in place of what has been sold, or in this case, raffled off. Either way, I'm always excited at the chance to redecorate, if you will."

"Do you have many other pieces that will go up?" Emily asked. She thought about the modern and abstract artwork she'd seen at Mr. Lowe's place, and she hoped Alfred had better taste.

"Oh, certainly," the gallery owner replied pleasantly as he rocked back and forth on his feet. "Some of what you've already seen in the side rooms, such as where the refreshments were before, was a bit crammed together to make room for the raffle. I have a few pieces in the back, as well. There will likely be a few other artists in town who'll be eager to get their work in here now that they know there's some space. In fact, I think I'll start arranging things now, if you'll excuse me."

"Of course."

A few guests were still lingering around as Emily and Lily began picking up the ticket bowls, chatting near the door, and comparing the paintings and sculptures they'd managed to win. Mr. Stevens seemed like a friendly man who ran a successful gallery, but his comments had her wondering. If artists were always clamoring to get their work in gallery, then could one of them have stolen the beautiful painting in order to boot Victor out of such a prestigious spot? Or could Alfred himself have slipped *Moonlight* out the back door one night in order to create a buzz around his gallery that would ensure his name got out in the news? She'd liked most of the other artists she'd met here, and she thought Mr. Stevens was also a rather genuine man, but there were certainly possibilities. Of course, her very first thought had been wrong. If Bert Lowe didn't steal Victor's painting, then who did?

The glass bowls clinked together in her hands as she gathered them up and brought them to the front table, where the tickets would be counted, and the shelter would get the money that had gone into them. She grumbled at the small pile, thinking that it didn't amount at all to what *Moonlight* would've brought in on its own. She picked up one of the tickets and turned it over to look at the name and phone number on the back. Maybe, just maybe, if she called every single of the ticket holders for that particular raffle, she could convince them to go ahead and donate their useless ticket price to the shelter instead of taking it back. It would take forever to get through them all, but she would do it for the sake of all the cats and dogs that could be saved.

Setting down the bowls, she moved across the room and paused when she heard Victor Elliott's demanding voice coming out of the long, narrow room at the side of the building where she'd helped put up a refreshment table a week ago.

"You've got to raise the price on this!"

"That's not a good idea," Alfred replied calmly. "It'll get more attention once we move it out of this room and back into the main gallery."

"But that's exactly why it should have a bigger price tag," the painter spluttered. "Nobody has seen it in here, but once you put in in the main room everyone will be breaking down the doors to get it. You can't deny that my name has been in the news a lot lately."

Alfred sighed. "Victor, that may be true, but it's also true that this particular painting of yours has been in the gallery for six months and I haven't had a single inquiry on it. It simply doesn't have the verve and luminescence of *Moonlight in her Hair.* It's almost as though they were created by two different artists."

Emily clutched the bowl to her chest, knowing she should move on. None of this was her business, but she was terribly curious. Any business owner would want to make as much money as possible, and she could presume that Alfred made a commission based on how much the artworks in his gallery sold for. Why wouldn't he want to increase the price on Victor's painting?

"You're in the industry. You know that artists go through different movements. Where would Picasso have been without his Blue Period?" Victor argued.

The older men let out an impatient sigh. "You're right. I *am* in the industry, and I also know that Picasso had a terrible time trying to sell the paintings from his Blue Period. Some things take time, and perhaps at some point someone will come along and be absolutely desperate for this painting of yours. That time is not now, and I'm not increasing the price. Now, I've got things to do." Victor breezed out of the room with a framed canvas in his hands, straight past Emily and toward the back wall of the main gallery.

She busied herself with the tickets until he'd left the room once again, presumably to fetch more paintings, but once she was in the clear, she couldn't help but coming over to see the painting for herself. Emily had to agree with Alfred's assessment, even though she was no expert when it came to art. The landscape wasn't badly painted, but it simply wasn't very exciting. The price tag on the corner of the frame was perhaps not as much as Victor wanted it to be, but it was certainly more than she'd be willing to pay to have such a thing hanging in her house.

Unsure of what else to do, Emily returned to the table and began counting the tickets.

CHAPTER SEVEN

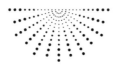

Cold rain drizzled down the back of Emily's neck, making her wish she'd bothered to get her umbrella out of the car instead of trying to make the short mad dash from the street and up to the Daydream Café. She ducked under the awning just as the downpour increased, sending a flood of water through the gutter. The scent of warm muffins beckoned to her as she moved toward the door of the little restaurant.

The door opened, and Alyssa Bradley emerged with a to-go cup of coffee in her hand. A little wisp of steam escaped from the hole in the top, and she smiled as she recognized Emily. "Well, if it isn't my favorite troublemaker!"

Emily laughed as she put an arm around her. "I guess I'm certainly that, aren't I? I was quite surprised when I didn't see you at Bert Lowe's place. You tend to show up everywhere I go, although I guess that doesn't say much for me."

Alyssa beamed at her. "I had the day off, but I felt terrible when I found out you were there. I hope Chief Inspector Woods didn't give you too much trouble."

Emily shook her head. "He was much too interested in the collection of stolen art than a couple of old ladies who'd stuck their noses where they don't belong. I think I heard him say this discovery was going to be the highlight of his career, and he didn't really bother with us very much after this."

"Yes, I could see that," Alyssa replied with a nod. "The stolen artwork is a huge deal, but

I'm afraid we're not really any closer on what actually happened to Mr. Lowe."

"I've been wondering about that myself," Emily admitted. "I've been spending a lot of time on my blog to distract myself from it. You see, I went to Mr. Lowe's place because I thought he might've stolen the painting from the gallery across the street. It wasn't there, so I was wrong. I can't say that I really have any idea as to who might've wanted to kill Mr. Lowe, but it's definitely bothering me."

Alyssa had a thoughtful look on her face as she shifted her coffee cup to the other hand. She glanced around, but the deluge of rain was keeping anyone from trying to go in or out of the café at the moment. "I'm afraid the department isn't very far ahead of you on that. It seems that the stab wounds were made with an oddly shaped object, not a regular knife. There was also a lot of mica powder found on the victim."

"Mica powder?" Emily had no idea what that was.

"It's a very shiny mineral that's ground up and put into all sorts of things. It's what makes eyeshadow all shiny and glittery, for instance. With the sheer number of products that it goes into, it doesn't narrow things down very much for us," Alyssa explained. "Other than the fact that there was a lot more of it than we would've expected, of course."

"How strange," Emily murmured. In fact, that statement could sum up the entire past week for her. She watched as the rain lifted as suddenly as it'd arrived, nearly stopping all together. The door behind Alyssa swung open as a woman stepped out of the café. She glanced toward the street before she moved off down the pavement. Was that the same woman she'd seen at the country club and at the drawing? She was walking swiftly enough that she was already too far away for Emily to chase her down, and Emily still hadn't figured out why she looked so familiar.

"Yes, it really is quite strange," Alyssa agreed.

"And what about the missing painting? *Moonlight in her Hair?*" Emily urged. She'd recently read about how many people over the years had become obsessed with the *Mona Lisa* for one reason or another, and she was starting to wonder if something similar was happening to her. It was a bunch of pretty paint on a piece of canvas, and yet she felt as though she wouldn't really be able to feel settled again until the painting was recovered. Even if they didn't get it back but were able to discover what'd happened to it, she'd feel much better. "Have you made any progress on that?"

"That's not a case that I'm on," Alyssa admitted. "I can check on it when I go into the office this afternoon, though."

"Thank you so much. You're a wonderful girl, Alyssa. If you hear anything you think I should know, give me a shout!"

When they said goodbye, Emily headed into the Daydream Café. It was a fairly new establishment to Little Oakley, but it didn't seem to be having any trouble getting enough business. Most of the little tables were busy, and there was a long line at the counter.

"Ah, there you are!" Alfred said from a back corner, waving his hand in the air. "I took the liberty of ordering you a coffee and a doughnut so you wouldn't have to wait in line."

"That was very kind of you." Emily sat down in front of the waiting drink and treat. "I have to admit, I'm desperate to know what you wanted to see me about. You were very vague on the phone this morning."

Mr. Stevens gave her a wide grin. "I had to be, because the news I have for you is simply too big to share over the phone. First, I'll tell you that my original reason for contacting you was because I wanted to enlist your help in planning a new show at the gallery. You did an excellent job for the shelter, and people seem to like you."

Emily paused as she added a bit of creamer to her coffee. "Really? Well, I'm very flattered! I'm happy to take on the job, but you should know that I'm not an expert."

"And how does one become an expert except through experience?" Alfred said with a laugh. "Now, the new show was going to be something rather simple, basically an invitation to the public to come in and see what the gallery has to offer now that the raffle is over."

"Yes?" Emily felt the steam of her coffee on her face as she leaned forward, eager to know what this exciting news was all about.

As Alyssa had done, Alfred glanced around to see if anyone was listening. They were in the back corner of the café, and everyone seemed to be involved in their own conversations. Even so, he lowered his voice as he leaned forward. "I came to work an hour ago, all prepared to get set up for the show I was telling you about. I always come in the back door, because I park my car in the alley back there. I see a canvas wrapped in a tarp sitting by the step. I think, 'Oh, some shy artist who doesn't want to be let down has left this here in the hopes that I'll display it, but it's probably terrible.' And what do you think it actually was when I removed the tarp?"

"No." Emily knew, but she definitely didn't want to be wrong. Not this time.

"Yes! *Moonlight in her Hair!* As beautiful as the day she was stolen! I couldn't believe it! I called Victor, and then I called the police. I had scarcely finished up with everyone right before I needed to come over here and meet you."

Emily leaned all the way against the back of her chair, her doughnut and coffee completely forgotten for the moment. "Do they have any idea what happened?"

The gallery owner shook his head emphatically. "They took some photos, and they dusted for fingerprints, but they didn't find anything conclusive. They said we should be grateful that it turned out this way, because most stolen property doesn't get recovered."

Her stomach rumbled, reminding her of the delicious pastry in front of her. She took a bite and tried to understand how she'd gone from lamenting over the missing painting a few minutes ago to rejoicing in its mysterious return. Why, she'd only asked Alyssa about it right before she'd come into the café! Her heart soared when she realized what the arrival of the painting meant. "The shelter is going to get all that money from the raffle now!"

"Yes, exactly!" Even Alfred couldn't hold back his enthusiasm. "I couldn't think of a better way to celebrate than with a big show at the gallery featuring Victor's work. He assures me that he has enough finished canvases to make it happen, although I might need to help out a bit with framing and mounting. That's not a problem at all; I do that sort of thing all the time for my artists. We'll put *Moonlight* back on display for the public for a limited time only. Then we'll be able to hold the drawing to see who gets to take it home, and perhaps Victor will sell a few other pieces in the process. It doesn't get any better than this, especially since I have you to help me arrange it all!"

Emily felt completely flabbergasted. "Yes, of course! When do you want to do this?"

"Two days. I know," he said as he held up his hands. "It doesn't give us very much leeway. I don't want to waste a second more than I have to before we can make the big reveal to the public. Victor and I will be putting in a lot of hours to make sure it all comes together."

"Then I suppose I'd better get started and put some hours in of my own." Feeling excited, Emily started to get up. She paused. "Wait! Does Lily know yet? She'll be absolutely delighted!"

"I haven't spoken to her yet, as I didn't want to run late for our meeting. Would you like to be the one who calls her?"

Emily had so much excitement spinning inside her already that she wasn't sure she could handle any more of it. There was no way she was going to pass up an opportunity like that, though. "I'll do one better and I'll go over there myself. Right now. Thank you again!" Grabbing the last bite of her doughnut, Emily drove straight over to the shelter.

The rain had started back up again, but Emily no longer cared if it dripped down her collar or made her hair a little extra frizzy today. She burst into the front door of Best Friends Furever, still filled to the brim with excitement. "Lily! Lily! I think I might explode before I get a chance to tell you!"

Lily's dark eyes widened as she looked up from the adoption applications she was sifting through. "What is it? Whatever it is, it must be awfully good!"

"Oh, it is. It's the most fantastic thing ever. I had coffee with Mr. Stevens, and he told me the good news. *Moonlight in her Hair* has been returned to the gallery!" She clasped her hands in front of her, reeling with delight.

Lily's knuckles turned white where she gripped the edge of the counter. "Are you sure? Because I don't think I could handle finding out that it wasn't actually true. I've been going over all the figures with what money we already made from the raffle, and it'll take me forever to get an addition without that painting."

"You don't have to wait forever," Emily assured her. "Only a couple of days. Mr. Stevens has a whole event planned out that will feature *Moonlight* and showcase the rest of Victor's paintings. He's even asked me to do the refreshments, which is so flattering I don't even know how to describe it."

"And then he'll hold the raffle?" Lily's eyes were shining with hope.

"Yes, he will! If I were you, I'd call up that friend of yours in construction and tell him to start drawing up the blueprints!" She let out a happy sigh as she looked around the familiar building where she'd spent at least a few hours a week volunteering for the last several months. Some things would have to change to make room for the new space, and it would probably be a bit of a logistical problem to deal with the animals while it was happening, but it was all going to be worth it in the end.

"Oh, Emily! I think I'm going to cry!" Lily fanned her face in an effort to stop the tears. "It's wonderful. It's absolutely the best news I've ever heard, but I can't help but wonder why all this happened. Why would someone steal the painting if they were going to return it?"

And why did Mr. Lowe get murdered somewhere along the way? Emily had plenty of questions in her own mind, but there was no time to fuss over them now. "There's nobody who wants to get down to the bottom of a good mystery more than I do, Lily, but right now I think we have to count our blessings. I'm going to run home and start planning. I'll be making a grocery list a mile long, I'm sure! You call me if you need anything!"

She bustled out the door and headed home. As the thrill of the returned painting began to abate a little, Emily's mind began to wander back to other matters. How, really, did the painting get returned? What happened to it in the first place? Did the theft actually have anything to do with Mr. Lowe's death, or was it purely coincidence? Would she ever find out the truth? She still wanted to know the answers, but for the moment she had to focus on her planning. Those hors d'oeuvres weren't going to make themselves!

CHAPTER EIGHT

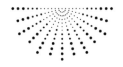

"Well, what do you think?" Emily turned this way and that, inspecting the champagne pantsuit she'd put on in the mirror.

Rosemary sat on the corner of the dresser, watching her owner. She reached out with one soft paw and batted the hem of the jacket.

"I know. It's a little bland compared to what I normally wear, but I didn't want anything that would clash with my hair too much. Tonight is all supposed to be about the paintings, after all, so I decided something a little more neutral would be appropriate." Emily opened her jewelry box for a pair of earrings, picking out a pair of dark sapphires that reminded her of the featured artwork this evening. "You know, Sebastian got these for me. I miss him all the time, but it was so strange to see that couple at the country club. The Dillons, yes, that was their name. I guess I was hoping they'd want to reminisce about Sebastian with me. That was a little ridiculous, wasn't it? They don't know me, and they hadn't known Sebastian for very long."

Rosemary butted her head up under Emily's hand, rubbing her kinked whiskers along the side of her owner's hand.

Emily obliged and scratched her between the ears. "Yes, I know I have you. I always do, don't I, dear? I feel as though I've been neglecting you a bit over the last couple of weeks, what with all this drama that's been going on at the gallery and such. At least you get some time to sit in my lap when I work on my blog, and there's been no shortage of material for that lately! In fact, tonight will probably give me even more to write about!" She smiled in the mirror as she put her earrings on. Though her readers hadn't taken to her current subject of party planning and fundraising in quite the way she would've hoped, Emily was enjoying it. She was learning something useful for herself and for the future of the shelter, and that could never be a bad thing.

When there was nothing further she could do to get ready for the evening, Emily headed downtown. She was grateful that the rain they'd had over the last few days had abated, so at least she didn't have to worry about the food getting wet.

"Ah, Ms. Cherry!" Mr. Stevens enthused as she hustled in the front door with a big, covered tray of canapes. "What can I do to assist you?"

She smiled at him, but she waved away his offer. "I'm sure you have plenty on your plate, and I'm supposed to be the one taking care of this part of things, after all. My, but you've made the place very lovely this evening!"

"Thank you so very much. I do try." He beamed as he looked around.

Emily knew she needed to get set up, but she allowed herself a moment to just soak in the feel of the place. Painted canvases had been framed and hung on the walls, grouped by subject. Over here there were landscapes, a series of portraits over there, and even some abstracts along the back wall. The overhead lights had been dimmed, but the spotlights on each individual painting had been turned up to increase the focus on the artwork. Off to the left stood a blank canvas, and a small table next to it held paints and brushes.

In the very center of the room was *Moonlight in her Hair.* Breathlessly, Emily stepped forward to examine it. Whatever had happened to it in the few days it was missing, at least it seemed to have been kept in good condition. It was exactly as she remembered it, and maybe it was even more special now that it'd gone missing. She studied the thin metallic lines that Victor had created to show the way the moon's light reflected in the subject's hair. It was absolutely fascinating, and it made her wish she had even a shred of that kind of talent.

"Fabulous, isn't it?" Lily said at her elbow. "I haven't been able to stop looking at it ever since I got here. I'm desperate to know who won it."

Emily looked down at the bowl. As before, it was full to the brim with tickets. Had someone taken the painting because they realized how little of a chance they had of actually winning the raffle? "Someone who's very lucky, indeed. I see that Finnegan is your constant companion these days. I'm surprised he hasn't been adopted yet." She smiled down at the dog, who sat alert and obedient at her feet.

"He could be," Lily admitted with a sigh. "There's been so much interest in him, but that's exactly the problem! With so many stellar applications, how do I choose the right person?"

Emily juggled her tray to one hand so that she could scratch Finnegan's head. "Maybe he'll be the one to choose."

The dog's tail thumped eagerly on the floor as Mr. Stevens strolled through the room with a canvas in his hands.

Emily raised her eyebrows meaningfully at Lily. "I'd better go get all this taken care of. I think we'll be opening the doors soon, and I don't want to be late!" She rushed into the refreshment area.

The small amount of time she had to set up breezed by, and soon the gallery was full. Emily was sure that everyone who'd purchased a raffle ticket for this particular painting had shown up, and probably a lot of people who were simply curious. That could only be good for Victor's sales, and he was currently preening for the media.

"Thank you all very much for coming," he said once Mr. Stevens had gotten everyone's attention and handed the floor to him. He'd traded out his shabby suit for one that didn't have threads hanging off the cuffs, and he tugged at the front of the jacket as he saw how many people had shown up with cameras. It wasn't just the press this time, but layfolk as well, who wanted to hear what he had to say. "Both Mr. Stevens and I are absolutely delighted to have you all here today. As you know by now, *Moonlight in her Hair* was miraculously returned, and it's a thrill worthy of a big celebration."

He paused as several people clapped and cheered.

"I know you're all anxious to get the drawing under way so you can find out which lucky person will be able to hang this in their living room, but I'd like to make a secondary announcement." Victor's eyes gleamed as he looked over the crowd. "*Moonlight* has been blessed with such a loving reception, and I truly enjoyed trying to capture such a celestial moment. That's why it will now be known as the first in a series. None of them will be quite the same, of course, as I believe each painting should have its own space and personality, but all of them will be based on the beautiful figure you see right here before you."

Another round of applause thundered through the room, one that clearly pleased both Victor and Mr. Stevens. Emily noted them beaming with pride, and she decided they must've put aside their earlier spat about the price of Victor's paintings now that they both knew they had a good chance of making money.

"And for those of you who decided to be here tonight, you're lucky enough that you get to see me start the first one!" Victor stepped away from *Moonlight* and toward the blank canvas nearby. He picked up a paint palette. "I have everything here to create a beautiful series of paintings that I think you'll all enjoy."

"Oh, no, you don't!" A tall, thin woman emerged from the crowd and marched straight up to Victor. She yanked the paintbrush out of his hand and snapped it in half on her thigh. Everyone gasped and took a step back, even Emily.

"Corinne!" Victor exclaimed, fear blanching his skin. "What are you doing here?"

"Stopping you, of course!"

"Please." Alfred Stevens stepped out, putting his palms out in an effort to placate her. "The two of you can have your lovers' spat some other time, but right now is not a good one."

"This is not a lovers' spat!" Corinne hissed. "I broke up with him three months ago!"

Emily studied the long, thin lines of her face, the way her chin had that odd but exotic angle. This was the same woman she'd seen at the country club party, and again at Daydream. She hadn't been able to pinpoint where she'd seen her before, but now that the comparison was literally right in front of her face, there could be no doubt.

"Yes, exactly," Victor spluttered. "You did, which means you have no business being here and ruining my show."

Corinne's arm flung out to the side, and Victor flinched. But she simply extended a long finger toward the painting in the center of the room. "I have every right to be here, considering you painted that picture of me!"

Another gasp rose up from the crowd, this time accompanied by speculation.

"My goodness! It *is* her!"

"I'll bet she was the one who stole the painting in the first place!"

"And then she returned it so she could come and make a spectacle. What a shame!"

Emily's eyes and ears were trying to take it all in. The subject of the painting wasn't someone she'd considered before, especially since

Victor had claimed he'd created the image from his own dream.

"I asked your permission," Victor said pointedly. The fear had left his face, and now it was replaced by annoyance. "You can't stand here and pretend you didn't know anything about it."

"That's not what I'm doing at all. You'd know that if you were listening, but you never do! That painting was supposed to be only for you. You told me all that dreamy romantic stuff to get me to pose for it, insisting it would never leave your home. Then you put it right in here on display for all the world to see."

Victor's jaw was tight. "It was for a charity! I didn't want it anymore, all right? I didn't need something hanging on my wall that constantly reminded me of you, no matter how good of a job I'd done on it. The sales will go straight to helping local cats and dogs. Isn't that right, Mr. Stevens?"

The gallery owner looked distinctly uncomfortable as his eyes bounced back and forth between Victor and Corinne. Beads of sweat stood out on his forehead, but he gestured vaguely at Lily and Finnegan. "Yes! Yes, of course! The money will all be handed over tonight!"

Now that long finger Corinne had used to point at her portrait jutted straight up under Victor's chin. "Is that your strategy? You try to make me look heartless so I'll be thrilled about all the work you've done here? This painting can go to whoever wins it, and I decided over a week ago there was nothing I could do about that. But the rest of this series is absolutely not happening!" She was still holding the broken halves of the paintbrush, and now she stabbed one of them through the blank canvas.

"How could you do that?" Victor snagged the brush from her hands, but Corinne wasn't willing to let go of it. She yanked backward, her elbow knocking into the table that held the other paint supplies. Several tubes of paint went sliding to the floor. Victor lunged at her again, and she stepped back quickly to avoid him. Her shoe came straight down on a tube of paint. The cap flew off and a squirt of bright blue shot out onto the floor.

"My carpet!" Mr. Stevens cried out, pressing his hands on either side of her head. "Stop it! Stop it right now!"

But the former couple wouldn't hear any of it. In fact, they seemed to be completely oblivious of how much of a scene they were making as they grappled with each other. Corinne was reaching for Victor's throat. "You don't have any right to build your reputation off my image!"

He held her arms at bay by grabbing her biceps. "Were you the one who stole the painting? Just to spite me?"

She was a strong woman, and she had him twisting from side to side as he tried to evade her. "I didn't steal your stupid painting, but I would have if I thought it would make you admit you're wrong for once!" Corinne's hip bumped into the edge of the table, and the rest of the supplies went tumbling. Brushes, palette knives, paints, cups, and jars rained down onto the floor, causing Mr. Stevens even more distress.

Emily was speechless as she watched the whole thing unfold, feeling frozen in place. She stared as a small plastic jar bounced to the floor. Its lid went flying, sending a cascade of golden powder out onto the carpet near the splatter of blue paint. It was as though *Moonlight in her Hair* was being recreated right there on the floor as a palette knife swirled through the mess. Ideas were quickly forming in her head.

Two men surged forward from the crowd. One of them wrapped his big arms around Corinne's waist and hefted her easily into the air as he stepped away. The other snagged Victor by his arms and pulled him in the opposite direction, breaking up the fight.

"Thank you," Mr. Stevens said breathlessly. "Just look at my carpet!"

Emily felt that she was finally able to move again as the men hauled Victor and Corinne into opposite corners of the room. She knelt down, carefully picking up tools and putting them back on a tray. "Don't worry, Mr. Stevens. I'm sure I can get this right out for you. I'll work on it while it's fresh."

The gallery owner was still completely distraught. He flung his hands in the air as he tried to compose himself. "You're a blessing, Ms. Cherry!"

She smiled up at him. "You get the rest of this party underway and leave this to me."

"Yes, of course. Ladies and gentlemen, I'm so sorry for that interruption. I'm afraid there won't be a live demonstration of Mr. Elliott's talent tonight, but we can still choose the winner for this painting. Ms. Austin, would you and Finnegan do the honors?"

Lily stepped forward with the dog in tow, and a ticket was chosen. "Sophia Wilkinson!" she announced.

While many people sagged their shoulders and let out disappointed noises, Sophia stepped forward with a smile on her face. Emily recognized her as one of the women who worked at Little Oakley Realty. She'd even interviewed her for her blog, discussing the topic of returning to work after retirement. She was dressed as brightly as she was before, her bright green skirt and scarf standing out against her deep purple blouse. "Oh, this is fantastic! Just excellent!" she said as she shook the hands of Mr. Stevens and Lily.

"Congratulations," Alfred said enthusiastically. "I know there were a lot of people who were interested in winning this painting. Do you have a few words you'd like to say?"

Looking as happy as if she'd won the lottery, Sophia nodded as she turned to the crowd. "I certainly do. It's easy to see by the number of tickets in that jar how many people were excited about this painting, and I'm thrilled that so much money was raised for Best Friends Furever. I know how badly they needed it. That's exactly why I'm donating this painting back to the shelter, so that it can be raffled off again."

The press and the public went wild, cheering and asking questions.

Emily's heart warmed as she worked on cleaning up the horrid mess on the floor. The night might have been a little bit of a disaster after the fight between Victor and Corinne, and there was a chance that Mr. Stevens might never want to put Victor's work in his gallery again. The shelter would get the funds they needed as well as a guarantee at even more, and that was what truly mattered to her.

She mopped up as much of the paint as she could with a napkin and then picked up the little jar of golden powder. It'd already gotten everywhere, and it was so finely ground that when it stuck to her fingers it looked more like paint than glitter. She realized this must be what Victor used to create the metallic look in his paintings. It was a very clever idea, but her mind was churning once again.

Glancing around, Emily saw that everyone's attention was on Sophia and the painting. She stuck her finger into the jar, coating it in gold before she wiped it off on the inside of her pocket. Emily was already starting to get some idea of what might've happened with the missing painting and murdered art thief, but there was only one way to find out for sure. She stepped into the back to find some water and cleaner to attack the paint spot with, taking a moment while she was back there to call Alyssa.

CHAPTER NINE

"I t's a picture of a pony," Lucy said proudly.

Alfred Stevens nodded patiently as he looked at her artwork. He held one end of Finnegan's leash, but he only needed to hold onto it with two fingers. The dog stayed obediently at his side, watching him for cues as they made their way around room.

Lucy twisted up her mouth and rolled her eyes to the ceiling. "Um, Rose?"

"That's a beautiful name for a pony, and it's a very beautiful picture, too. I'm very pleased to have it on display here. Thank you so much for donating your work to such a wonderful cause."

"Thanks, um, can I pet your dog?" Lucy pointed at Finnegan.

Mr. Stevens laughed. "Of course you can!"

Emily let out a long whoosh of breath. She hadn't been certain that coming back to the Stevens Fine Art Gallery would be a good idea, but when Lily and Alfred had come to her with their idea, she simply couldn't say no. There had to be another raffle in order for the shelter to benefit from Sophia Wilkinson's generous donation, but Alfred hadn't been too certain about working with the same kinds of artists again. Instead, local children had done drawings of their favorite animals and donated them to the cause. They now stood proudly next to their artwork.

"Mr. Stevens, this is wonderful," Emily gushed. "I know my granddaughters are thrilled, and I think the other children are, too. Having their work displayed in a fine gallery like this has got to be quite the feather in their caps!"

He laughed again, back to his normal self now that he wasn't watching his gallery be destroyed. "They're much better behaved than some adults are! And honestly, these drawings and paintings are precious. Everything from crayon to watercolor, and so much enthusiasm! It warms my heart beyond belief!" He clutched his free hand to his chest.

Lily stepped over to them, holding a tuxedo cat with a harness in her arms. "Mr. Stevens, I hope you're prepared to do more events like this! It's going to be a huge success. The bowl is practically full again for *Moonlight in her Hair,* and it looks like the young artists are bringing in quite a haul of their own."

"I will, but only as long as the two of you agree to help me out! You're excellent party planners!" he gushed.

Emily waved way his praise. "I don't know about that. I'll always do what I can to help the shelter. Animals are near and dear to my heart, but I think my actual party planning days are over! I don't want to see another canape for at least a week, or maybe a month."

Lily's smile was so wide she looked like she could barely contain herself. "I forgot to thank you, Mr. Stevens, for inviting some of the shelter animals to come to the event tonight. The children love it, of course, but I've also had grown-ups put in quite a few applications. It makes a huge difference when people can actually see the animals we have available."

"Don't I know it?" Alfred ruffled Finnegan's ears. "I never knew I needed a dog until I met this gentleman here, and he's been coming to work with me every day. I swear, he loves the paintings as much as I do, and he's going to be the world's first canine art critic. As for letting them in, well, I figured the carpet was ruined anyway." He let out another big laugh.

Emily gazed down at the blue spot on the floor. She'd managed to make it better, but it was never going to be quite the same again.

She'd been worried for Alfred over it, but he seemed to have made his peace with it.

She spotted a familiar face making her way through the young artists. Alyssa Bradley knelt down in front of Ella to get on eye-level. "Hi. I love your drawing."

"You do? You like kitties?" Ella's eyes lit up.

Alyssa nodded at the swirling scribbles on the page displayed behind the little girl. "I do, and I especially like yours. I think I'm going to put two tickets in your bowl, because I'd love to have that on display in my office."

Ella's mouth about dropped open as she watched the tickets go in. Her eyes shot up and met Emily's. "Gran! I got *two* tickets! She gave me two tickets!"

Emily chuckled at her sweet granddaughter, thinking that young artists were definitely better behaved than older ones. "I see that! How very exciting! Make sure you tell her thank you."

"Thank you!" Ella wrapped her arms around Alyssa's neck. "Thank you, thank you!"

"Aw, you're very welcome." Alyssa hugged her back. "Do you mind if I talk to your gran for a minute?"

Emily was simmering with warmth and pride as she and Alyssa stepped out of the main gallery and into the refreshments room. She'd laid out a wide assortment of foods, but this time they hadn't needed to be nearly as fancy. "Would you like a biscuit?"

"Yes, thank you. I have some information I wanted to share with you, and I knew you'd be here today. It didn't make sense to try to call you, but I hope you don't mind if borrow a little bit of your time."

"Not at all." Emily peeked out into the main gallery, not wanting to leave her granddaughters alone, but she saw that they were under the watchful eye of both Alfred and Lily, and she wasn't worried. "I'm glad you're here, and I know the girls appreciate your donations."

"They're darling," Alyssa beamed. "I thought you'd be interested to hear that we've found out a little bit more about Bert Lowe."

Emily had done what she could with what little information she had, and she'd done her best to try to leave it in the hands of the police ever since. It hadn't been easy, and she knitted her fingers together as she waited. "Yes! Please, tell me."

"We've taken a deep dive into Mr. Lowe's finances, as well as his associations, and it's been rather interesting. He was known for being a high-end art broker, and he really did conduct a legitimate business that way. There are people all over town who've purchased from him, and we've been able to verify that those works were both bought and sold legally, and that they're authentic.

"However," she continued, "the rest of the art that was found in the hidden room was absolutely on the black market. It sounds as though he'd taken to stealing a few small things here and there when their owners refused to sell them, or when he had a client who was willing to pay a handsome sum for something that couldn't legally be moved. After a while, he started doing it simply for the pleasure. A friend of his explained to us that Mr. Lowe did steal *Moonlight in her Hair,* but not because it was particularly valuable. It'd become a game for him, and he wanted to steal from a place that he hadn't had any experience with."

Emily realized her mouth was hanging open, and she snapped it shut. "I don't understand. At the time, the police said the painting was not at Mr. Lowe's studio."

"That's right." Alyssa picked up a cup of punch to wash down her cookie. "You see, Bert Lowe stole the painting, but then it was stolen from him. Victor had already planned to steal it before Mr. Lowe got his hands on it, and then he had to get it back."

"So, he killed Mr. Lowe?" she asked.

"Victor Elliott explained to us that he planned to steal the painting, but just long enough for it to generate some news and publicity. He'd been trying to make a name for himself in the art world for a long time, and he knew there were some paintings that hadn't become famous until they were stolen. He figured he'd make it go missing for a few days, lap up all the attention, and then his career would be made."

This made perfect sense to Emily, considering the way Victor had been arguing to raise the prices on his other paintings. He'd also made a comment about perhaps never painting again because he was so distraught over the theft. That would definitely drive up the price of his work, but only if people cared about it enough.

"He attempted to steal *Moonlight,* only to find that it was already gone," Alyssa continued. "Being in the art world, he had a good idea of who had it. Victor confronted Mr. Lowe in his studio, and there was a struggle. He hadn't meant to kill him, but he stabbed Mr. Lowe with the only thing he had in his pocket, a palette knife."

Emily chewed her bottom lip as she remembered the way the shiny metal tool had gone tumbling to the floor, and how much it'd made her wonder in the moment if she could possibly be on the right track. She'd doubted herself, and yet she'd been completely right. Even when it came down to suspecting Mr. Lowe of stealing *Moonlight,* she'd been correct. She'd have to remember to trust herself a little more in the future.

"And the mica powder that was found on Mr. Lowe's body?" Emily asked.

Alyssa nodded as she dabbed her mouth with a paper napkin. "An exact match with the dust from Victor's supplies you brought me. Apparently, it's used to mix with paint or other media to create a shiny, metallic look."

Emily was relieved to know that her efforts hadn't been wasted, but she had to laugh. "You should've seen the look on your face when I brought you a pocket full of shiny dust."

Alyssa laughed, too. "I'm sure. It wasn't the kind of thing I was expecting, but it was the clue that clinched the case. Victor was refusing to talk to us at all until we told him about the match, and then he cracked like a nut."

Though she'd had some of these suspicions herself, it was still hard to hear it all come out so simply. Emily knew that it'd taken a lot of police work and interviews to get down to the bottom of the story, and it'd certainly taken some work on her own part, but now it was all boiled down into a nice little package. "I'm glad that it's all over with. I know it caused a lot of stress both for myself and for Lily. She was really relying on that painting, and thanks to the generous winner its going to create quite a bit more income for her." She peered out into the gallery, where Lily was bending down to let one of the children pet the big cat in her arms.

"And what about you, Emily? I hear you've been putting on quite the parties lately. Are you going to come out of retirement to start organizing galas and arranging festivities?" Alyssa popped another cookie into her mouth.

Emily laughed again as she shook her head. "I'm no more likely to do that than I am to paint the next *Starry Night*. Unless we're raffling off watercolors of ponies and crayon drawings of cats, I think I'll find something else to occupy my time!"

THANK YOU FOR CHOOSING A PUREREAD BOOK!

We hope you enjoyed the story, and as a way to thank you for choosing PureRead we'd like to send you this free Special Edition Cozy, and other fun reader rewards...

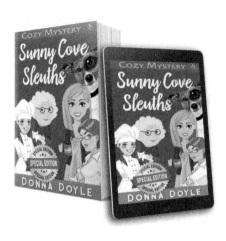

Click Here to download your free Cozy Mystery PureRead.com/cozy

Thanks again for reading.

See you soon!

OTHER BOOKS IN THIS SERIES

If you loved this story and want to follow Emily's antics in other fun easy read mysteries continue **dive straight into other books in this series...**

Read them all...

A Troubling Case Of Murder On The Menu

A Crafty Case Of Murder At The Fair

A Hairy Case of Murder At The Animal Sanctuary

A Clean & Tidy Case of Murder - A Truly Messy Mystery

A Cranky Case of Murder at the Autostore

OUR GIFT TO YOU

AS A WAY TO SAY THANK YOU WE
WOULD LOVE TO SEND YOU THIS
SPECIAL EDITION COZY MYSTERY
FREE OF CHARGE.

Our Reader List is 100% FREE

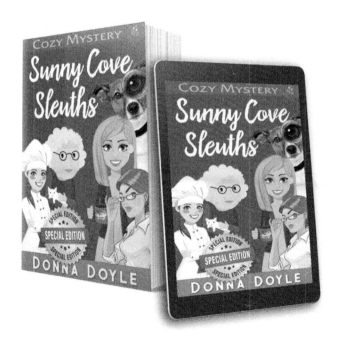

Click Here to download your free Cozy Mystery **PureRead.com/cozy**

At PureRead we publish books you can trust. Great tales without smut or swearing, but with all of the mystery and romance you expect from a great story.

Be the first to know when we release new books, take part in our fun competitions, and get surprise free books in your inbox by signing up to our Reader list.

As a thank you you'll receive this exclusive Special Edition Cozy available only to our subscribers...

Click Here to download your free Cozy Mystery **PureRead.com/cozy**

Thanks again for reading.
See you soon!

Printed in Great Britain
by Amazon